CHAOS CLOCK

GILL ARBUTHNOTT

Kelpies

Kelpies is an imprint of Floris Books
First published in 2003 by Floris Books
This second edition printed in 2013
Copyright © 2003 Gill Arbuthnott

Gill Arbuthnott has asserted her right under the
Copyright, Designs and Patents Act 1988
to be identified as the Author of this Work.

The publisher acknowledges subsidy from
Creative Scotland towards the publication
of this volume

 This book is also available
as an eBook

British Library CIP Data available
ISBN 978-086315-983-1
Printed in Poland